good deed rain

45 Books by Allen Frost

...Ohio Trio...Bowl of Water...
...Another Life...Home Recordings...
...The Mermaid Translation...The Selected Correspondence of Kenneth Patchen...
...The Wonderful Stupid Man...
...Saint Lemonade...Playground...Roosevelt...
...5 Novels...The Sylvan Moore Show...
...Town in a Cloud...A Flutter of Birds Passing Through Heaven: A Tribute to Robert Sund.......At the Edge of America.......
....Lake Erie Submarine....The Book of Ticks....
.........I Can Only Imagine.........
...The Orphanage of Abandoned Teenagers...
...Different Planet...Go With the Flow: A Tribute to Clyde Sanborn...Homeless Sutra...
..The Lake Walker..A Hundred Dreams Ago..
....Almost Animals....The Robotic Age....
....Kennedy....Fable....Elbows & Knees: Essays and Plays....The Last Paper Stars....
...Walt Amherst is Awake...When You Smile You Let in Light....Pinocchio in America....
....Florida....Blue Anthem Wailing....
...The Welfare Office...Island Air...
...Imaginary Someone...Violet of the Silent Movies....The Tin Can Telephone....
....Heaven Crayon....Old Salt....
...A Field of Cabbages...River Road...
....The Puttering Marvel....

the PUTTERING *MARVEL*

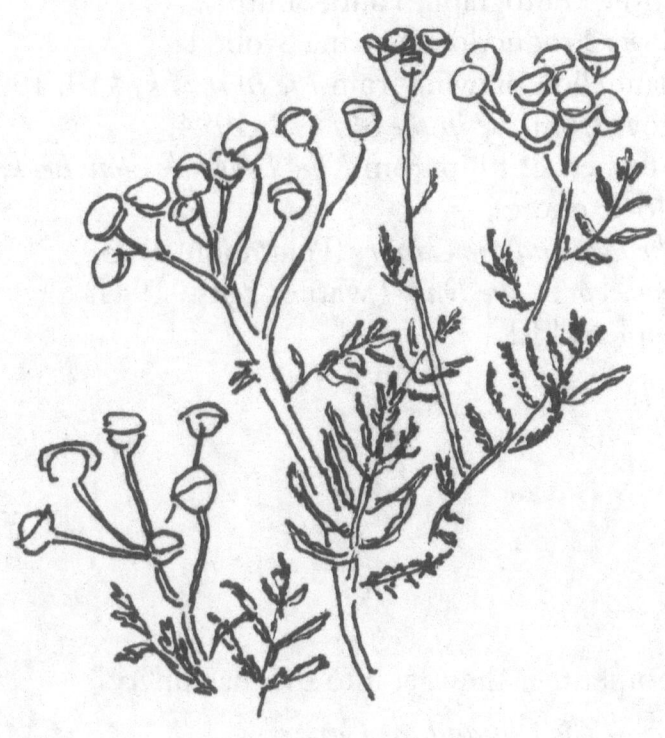

The Puttering Marvel ©2021
Allen Frost, Good Deed Rain
Bellingham, Washington
ISBN 978-1-63732-416-5

Writing & Drawings: Allen Frost
Cover Photograph: Laura Smith
Cover Production: Katrina Svoboda
Dandelion drawing from *Pie in the Sky* #19, 1993.
Stove from *Pie in the Sky* #78, 1994.
Pinwheel & tulip from *King Leopold's Slow Leak*, 2000.
Movie quotes:
The Cat and the Canary (Paramount, 1939)
Footsteps in the Dark (Warner Bros., 1941)
Apple: TFK!

"Sometimes they get into the machinery."
　—*The Cat and the Canary*

The Puttering Marvel

Allen Frost

Good Deed Rain ◊ Bellingham, Washington ◊ 2021

CONTENTS

The Puttering Marvel.................................... 9

The Broken Record...................................... 19

Holly.. 27

El Caminos.. 33

The Meanest Parents Ever............................ 39

Silent Movie Stars... 45

The Old Submarine...................................... 57

The New Apple Tree..................................... 63

Other Flavors.. 69

Wild Birds... 79

Marvelous Marvin's Unreal Estate................ 87

Afterword..93

THE PUTTERING MARVEL

My wife calls me a putterer. That word makes me sound like a little outboard motor though, as if all I do is make a wake out in the inlet going from wave to wave. I'd like the world to know I'm doing more than that. Below our house is a basement carved into the dirt. That's where I have my table saw and tools. I've made birdhouses, three rowboats, flower boxes and toys for the grandkids. Whatever catches my fancy.

Yesterday I started work on a nesting box. When the tide goes out, the inlet turns into a mudflat. That's when the blue heron goes hunting among the pools. My friend Jean calls him "walky-up-the-creeky" in honor of the way it feeds on the stream that runs into the bay. I'm hoping to get this big wooden nest into the tree that leans out over the beach. That would be something else to look out our bedroom window and see a pair of herons and their young. I've heard it's good luck to have them roost by your house. I would enjoy watching them too, seeing them swoop and flap and cackle like prehistoric flying things.

After lunch my wife cleared the plates and brought them to the sink. I finished my cigarette, stubbed it out in the metal boat-shaped ashtray. Sometimes I sit for a while and watch the birds on the feeder. I built that flat platform for them, also the one with suet attached to the tree trunk. I cut a hole in the coconut that hangs off a branch. It rattles with sunflower seeds. I haven't yet outsmarted the squirrels. I'll have to build something circus-proof.

I stood up and told my wife, "I'm going to work downstairs."

She was at the sink, filling the yellow plastic tub with hot soapy water. "Okay," she said and hummed to the song on the radio. Paul Harvey's news was over and now we knew the rest of the story.

I left the kitchen and the ancient oil stove that kept the room so warm. Every morning I lit the blue pilot light and it kept us company all day. By the door, I took my sweater off the pegboard, another one of my puttering jobs. The door I didn't make, but I did stain it so the maple glows like a moth wing.

Along the side of the house I followed the path crunching beneath my shoes. Blue and white mussel shells were crushed and scattered. Low tide leaves them strewn on the stone beach, readymade paving for our path. Broken shells lead to the shore and in the other direction uphill to the mailbox and our parked car.

Down a couple cement steps I stopped at the basement door. A horseshoe is nailed by the frame, good luck rusted to our house.

I'm not going to paint the nesting box. I think it should be kept natural as if it just happened to bloom on the pine tree crown like a flower.

I unclasped the padlock and gave the door a push. I always look forward to the damp cool and the smell of cut wood. Maybe I keep coming up with projects just so I can come back here. There's a kernel of truth there...maybe more than a kernel, maybe a whole stalk. As I reached into the dark for the light bulb drawstring, I thought of Jack's magic beanstalk growing in the sawdust, lifting our house a thousand feet off the ground. I imagined opening the door and the clouds waiting for me to walk on them.

I was already stepping down into the cellar, I couldn't stop my momentum even as I realized there was something huge waiting for me and the air was hot and humid as a swamp. Despite the sheer mass of the creature before me, it regarded me with tiny shining eyes. I knew what it was: my grandson never stops talking about dinosaurs and this was one of his favorites. Last Christmas I made him a stegosaurus out of pine and now here it was, come to life, big as a Volkswagen.

It snorted and the jagged plates on its back turned enough to easily knock the furnace over. Ductwork fell like guts to the floor.

Upstairs, I knew my wife would be on her way to see what made that crash.

The stegosaurus rocked its head and just missed one of the support beams. I had to act quickly, before it brought the house down.

I moved around the wall past the table saw, slushing through the piled sawdust. When I said I made three rowboats, I'm not the sort of absentminded carpenter who realizes he doesn't have a way to get his oversized creation out the door. No, I was steadily making my way to the carriage door.

The beast's thorned tail struck the furnace and crushed it like a tin can. I don't suppose our insurance will cover that—I'm sure a stegosaurus on the loose can probably be seen as an act of God. At last my hand felt over the latch and I heaved the panel door aside.

I figured the sunlight would be enough to draw it outside to the smell of forest and grasses. I was right about that but it lunged much faster than I expected. I only had a moment to step back from its clawed feet. I wasn't quick enough to avoid its shoulder, sideswiping me like a taxi cab as it tossed me aside and broke through the rest of the door and took some of the wall with it too. I lay on my side, holding my ribs, the wind knocked out of me, just out of the way of its thick tail dragging past. I remembered my grandson telling me it had a second brain back there somewhere under that armor and I thought of one of those long city fire trucks with the second driver whipping about the end.

"John!" my wife screamed. "What happened?" I saw her through a cloud of dust, bent support poles and hanging insulation. She stood in the open doorway I came through back before I ever expected a dinosaur. "Are you alright?"

I turned on my elbow. I could breathe again but it hurt, as if I had swallowed a saw. I was lucky my ribcage hadn't caved in. I couldn't tell Catherine to stay where she was. Who knew if she was any safer there or anywhere? Anyway, she hurried to my side and helped me get to my feet.

"What happened in here?" she asked, "What happened to the door?"

With difficulty, I said, "Dinosaur."

The woods echoed with a brassy roar and a tree snapping.

"It's heading for the water," I wheezed. I took a step out the torn wall and Catherine seized my arm.

"John, we can't, it's dangerous!"

"I know." I didn't want to miss it though. There may never be another dinosaur in my workshop. I sure hope not.

It was no mystery to see the way it went. I grabbed my axe from the chopping block as I stepped around the toppled stack of winter wood. I wasn't going to attack a stegosaurus with it; I wanted something to lean on. Catherine clung to my sweater like a drift anchor. I couldn't cut her loose though, not with that monster on the prowl. And oh didn't my ribs hurt, I was sure something must be cracked or sprained.

"There it is!" said Catherine and squeezed me again.

"Careful...I think something's broken."

"It looks like a dragon!"

Another tree, a birch, shattered and fell. The dinosaur was following the path, mowing down the brush that grew on either side, including our blueberries. The hill fell off a ten foot cliff. We had a narrow set of steps chiseled into the craggy wall, and a couple eye hooks strung with rope gave you something to hold. None of that would help a stegosaurus get to the shore. It bumbled on at a rate that would soon take it tumbling over the edge like a tractor.

"It's headed for the dock!" Catherine gasped.

It really was just like Godzilla, drawn to the Tokyo I spent all those days creating—a platform of oak planks, stilted and held aloft by driftwood logs cut and fitted like graceful bracing—targeted now by the beady eyes and hot breath aimed that way just so it could wreck it. There was no stopping it. I don't think its stubby legs could've changed its course if it wanted to.

Many a high tide the kids and I would sit on the end of that dock, legs dangling, watching the water underneath. I would bring a couple fishing poles and let them cast. You could catch a mackerel if they were running.

Before it reached that puttering marvel of mine, the dinosaur knocked over one last tree—the pine I planned to put my heron nesting box in. Maybe it was just trying to halt its avalanche, throwing its tail out to brake. Or maybe it just wanted to take as much of the world with it as it crunched onto the dock. I never built it to hold the weight of a stegosaurus. The driftwood legs snapped and down it went, crashing onto the beach with a slap.

A seagull shrieked across the mud.

I took Catherine's hand and we approached the cliff. At least we knew the dinosaur couldn't get back up the embankment. We had to get pretty close to the drop-off to see. Not too close though, we didn't need to take any more chances.

"Just look at it," Catherine sighed.

It looked pitiful, sunken in the stones and sand with the slack eelgrass tangling its feet. Its small head, no bigger than a greyhound's it seemed, stared back at us and it moaned. This was just like one of those monster movies I watch with my grandson. No matter how terrible the monster has been, you hate to see the agony of its end.

The stegosaurus heaved itself further from land. I don't know what it was thinking. Two brains or not, ahead of it was nothing but mud and that slender low tide channel. And with each step it took, that forklift weight of it punched it in deeper. It gave a hearty thrash as it reached the black thick tidal mud. I would warn the kids to never go out that far. I told them stories about the honeypots that were just like quicksand and just as fast to drag you under. It happened just like I said. The poor beast gave a terrible steam whistle cry and then it was gone. I heard that fearful screech echo across from the firs on the opposite shore.

I couldn't look at that tortured spot on the mud where it went down. It reminded me of the oil slicks I had seen in the water during the war.

Catherine helped turn me around. You couldn't see much of the house from where we were. We were lucky if it was still there. I told my wife I needed to get to the doctor. Maybe she could call Hap and Charley and see if they could do something about the hole in the basement, something temporary for the night. If my table saw wasn't broken, I could get some nice lumber delivered. I could make another wall. Being a putterer always gives me something new to do.

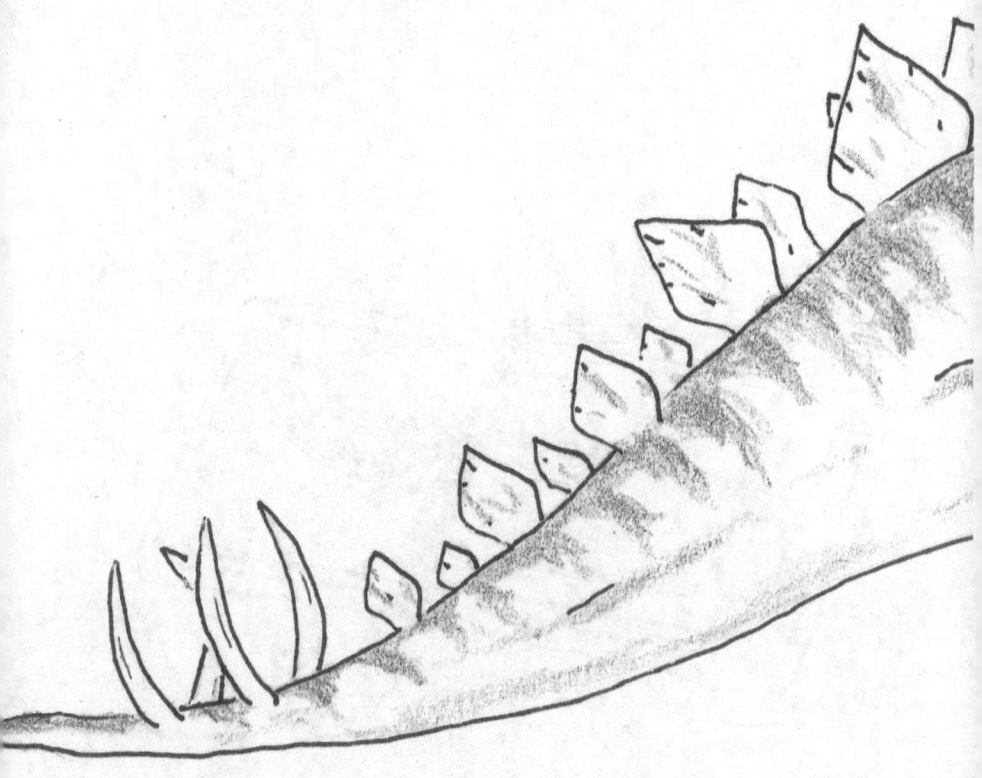

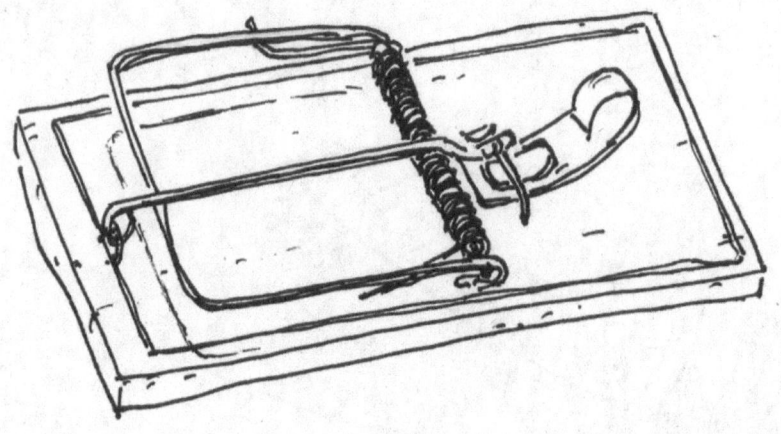

THE BROKEN RECORD

I told her always be very careful, you couldn't trust a coyote no matter how sweet it stared back at her like a stuffed animal toy. I told her the pack sent her that one she liked especially for her, they knew she would fall under its simple spell and she would follow it when it wanted to lead her back into the forest. That's what they do. It's the way they hunt. I reminded her that's how they got the neighbor's dog, just a puppy. I had to kneel down to her level and look her in the eye. That poor Labrador must have seen the same young coyote she did, a fluffy gray thing with its head bent down to play. And off it went, everyone wants a friend, and the woods are a fun place to run around.

The ferns waved. Just beyond them the leafy alders and the taller darker firs and cedars.

"You go inside now," I said and stood back up. I don't mind my daughter playing out here in the yard, but not when there's a coyote this close. She ran to the porch while I lit another cigarette. I know they're killers, but nothing in life is forever, is it? As long as I can breathe I don't mind.

I heard the screen door slam. She would soon be telling her mom all about what happened, how it wasn't fair, how I always told her not to do things she wanted to do. I know I was a broken record.

My eyes followed a cloud of drifting smoke. My truck was parked where it disappeared. The morning rain still sparkled on the tarp thrown over the cab. The roof's got a leak I need to fix one of these days.

The cigarette was halfway to my mouth again when I heard a gunshot, a sharp crack that boiled across the air. Then I heard a scream.

It wasn't a coyote. I know how they can trick you that way, but it was someone in pain, it came from the direction of the water.

Maybe someone was target shooting on the beach, or tripped carrying their gun.

I ran to the truck and tossed the wet tarp aside. The water ran down my sleeve and back towards my hand as I reached in my pocket for the key. In the door and slam, I fit the ignition and turned the key hurriedly. The engine roared, I threw it into gear and circled on the driveway. I have a first aid kit behind the seat. I've seen gunshot wounds before, usually just in deer.

The radio was playing a stupid song. As I spun the wheel onto the gravel road, I turned it off. This wasn't a rainy night and no use pretending it was something to love. The ocean wasn't far away. I could already see it through the trees. In the winter, the storms can carry the sound of the breakers clear to our door.

The road made a sharp last twist and ran straight at the sea. Tires shook on the rutted dirt. I had a clear view of the gray waves. The beach was littered with white driftwood, slung along the high tide line. Someone could be lying down hurt in that jumble. I pumped the brake and parked and jumped out, grabbing the kit from behind my seat before I shut the door.

It's almost like being underwater already, this close to the ocean you can breathe it, feel its pull on you and you realize how tiny you are compared, a little bit of silt ready to be picked up and carried away. I was running again, this time across the sand between patches of seagrass. The land becomes the sea in layers. Next I was crunching into stones the size of walnuts. I hopped onto a log pale as a whale bone and looked for any sign of someone injured. I yelled. My voice didn't seem to carry much further than the gulls crying off to the left. There were two of them, watching me.

This was a lonely place. Even the gulls were few. You got the feeling something bad happened here, some tragedy. It clung to the place like weeds or barnacles. When I was going through a bad time, I was drawn to this spot. I was almost here too much, staring at the horizon. Out there the sky meets the water like the rim of a glass. Part of me went missing and it never came back.

I don't know why I was so sure the gunshot came from here and the scream that came after. What if it was on the TV, a show that echoed off the trees? I don't know why I let myself fall for the worst. There was nothing on the beach but those gulls on my left and the wreck of an old boat crunched on shore. It's been there for years, like everything else shaped by the wind. It's just waiting for time to wear it down.

I was about to turn around and leave when I saw someone arise in that broken boat as if they had followed steps up from underground, right through the splintered hull. It was spooky.

But I stood there planted in the smoothed rocks, still holding onto that plastic first aid kit. I was close enough to feel the hook set, sharp and steely and with the tug that followed, I began to move. I knew who it was. In the back of my mind, he never went away. He was just the way I remembered him. That black coat of mine I gave him that he wore all that last winter. I ran the last bit of way there, scattering those chittering beach stones.

Do people that die really go away? I don't think so. They stick with you. Sure as a shadow they follow you wherever you go.

It was heartbreaking to see. My brother was only 23 when he drowned, exactly the way I remember him. Haven't I been through enough since then, when he died all those years ago? Somehow I made myself go on. And now it was worth it.

He laughed. Nobody could know how that cut me. He said, "Look at you! You're an old man."

I know I am, compared to what I was.

"I can still tell it's you though."

"It's me," I agreed and my voice hitched like a rusty piece of machinery. "You look the same," I managed. All I wanted to do was cry. When he stepped out of the boat and threw his arms around me, I did.

I don't know if he got some chance to come back, I don't know how it works on the other side. I was just so glad to see him again and know this wasn't another dream.

"Come on," he said. It was just like when we were kids, time had faded away. He said, "Hop on."

While I found a place on the broken bench, he pulled the bow across the rest of the shore and we were floating. How were we floating? The boat was full of holes. None of the shallow water seeped in. It paneled every scratch and wound like window glass. I could see the mottled sand and a ring of minnows.

He sat in front of me the way you would if you were rowing but there weren't any oars. Something else propelled us effortlessly. The waves pressed themselves flat before reaching us and shrugged around us as if they were afraid to touch our boat.

"Where are we going?" I said. I held on tighter than I wanted to the plank seat, my cold fingers felt nailed in.

"Don't worry." He wore a smile I didn't remember. Something about his teeth was wrong. It seemed that his mouth could barely keep them in. His shoulders under that black coat twisted, I saw his hands jump and cup together, hiding his nails.

I knew he wasn't my brother. How could he be? If only I could break the spell. If I could throw myself overboard, was there still time to get back ashore?

His eyes were black pearls as he repeated, "Don't worry." With a sharp grin he told me, "You can't believe how many people have died out here on the sea."

HOLLY

It's true that Buddy Holly is back, living in a boarding house about twenty minutes from the Canadian border. It's cold; it's not Lubbock, Texas. It took a while to get used to the new surroundings and the new body. And finding a guitar was essential as a seedling feeling for the sun. She had to have one. Holly got her first guitar when she was six. She heard the Beatles on the radio and played along. Everyone said she was a natural.

She got right to work writing her own songs. By the time Holly was 12, she had filled a box with cassette tapes. She found inspiration everywhere in everything. She was a sensitive girl, observant of seasons and feelings and the connections that linked all you see or didn't see. She must have known time was short; she didn't want to miss a thing.

One summer night she heard another music. She put her guitar down on the bed and went to the window.

The street had its own song of passing cars and crows. Wind chimes on the porch downstairs. A pigeon trying its best to impress paced the ledge. A dog barked behind a fence, laughter from a couple holding hands on the sidewalk. The sun was gone behind rooftops, the sky was painting itself violet and something new played in the distance. She remembered the posters she had seen on telephone poles and store windows. The fair was calling her, a rumble of a rollercoaster and the faint squeak of screams.

Every July the boardwalk became a fairground. Just for three nights. Last year she missed it, she was visiting her dad in Spokane.

With a wave she left her guitar, it was like leaving a friend behind for the night, knowing we'll see each other in a while. She put her sweater on and took her purse off its nail. She didn't know what she was walking into but she felt sure it would become another song.

The house was always creaking or sending out signals from other rooms. Even a ghost would have a hard time going down the wooden stairs without letting everyone know. She didn't expect to be gone for long, she didn't even leave her mom a note.

The streetlights were already on. The cars slid past on headlight beams.

The Bradley's cat sprinted across the sidewalk. It had killed every songbird that visited the backyard of the boarding house. Holly used to love being woken by them at 5 AM. She would listen until she fell back asleep. The cat ran round the corner of the house through the weeds.

On the corner in front of the little grocery, Mrs. Ramone was having a cigarette outside the door, one hand on the bin of oranges. She brightened when she saw Holly nearing and asked, "Where's the guitar?"

"I left it at home. I'm going to the fair."

"You be careful you don't lose all your money."

"I won't, Mrs. Ramone. I just want to see it up close and walk around."

Mrs. Ramone squinted and shook her head as if she had seen all she ever wanted to see of circuses and sideshows. Her little grocery with gold lit windows and rows of cans and fruits was all she needed.

Holly crossed the street. The boardwalk was only a few blocks away.

The Richardson's dog stopped barking and looked through the fence as Holly passed. Between the slats, she could see his nose and the flash of his wagging tail. They knew each other. She saw him every day, she even wrote a song about him. It was on one of those tapes in her room.

She wasn't the only one headed for the boardwalk. Other people were entranced. By now she could hear the music purring, a clatter of tin, and see the circus light above the trees squeezed like orange juice. Ahead of her on the next block marched a boy and girl holding hands. She wished for that electricity. If she found the right boy she would never let go of his hand.

A stairway crept down the embankment through a wall of blackberry. During the day, she would reach out for them, at night you might grab a thorn, or, on a night like this you could be bumped off by accident by some other kid running down the steps. They were like rapids flowing down the hill. If she had someone's hand to hold she would race too, clatter on the stairs, across the bridge over the railroad tracks, all the way to the chain link fence that surrounded the summer fair. This was something meant to share.

She reached into her purse, around her notebook and took out enough money to get through the gate. Amazing things awaited her—a funhouse, bumper cars, a man on stilts ten feet tall, pink cotton candy as big as her head—amazing and horrifying—a clown in a suit, long red tie, yellow fright wig who bellowed and boasted and urged the crowd to follow him into the sideshow alley. The music was blasting, bright neon lights glazed on her glasses, sizzling smells, everywhere was somewhere to stare, everything was all America rolled up in one.

Past the screams on the Octopus, another ride caught her eye. Fly Me to the Moon. Little tin airplanes lifted you into painted clouds. She got another dollar, the line wasn't bad, and before she knew it a boy helped her onto the red painted seat of her very own silver plane. He even gave her a wink. This could be the song I was looking for, Holly thought. A little bit of melody came her way already, it was humming just ahead.

The track jolted and the airplanes in front of her were taking off, going up the clattery track that led to a dark space cut in the painted clouds. One by one they disappeared. She waved to the happy faced moon outlined in colored light bulbs and that was the last Holly saw of this world. As she entered the darkness, her little plane shook and tilted to the right. She screamed, she couldn't help it, and she held on tight as she spun. Flames shot just over the wing, another violent shake and then blinding white light.

Silence. Holly pulled herself out of the airplane crash. Where were the others, where were the tracks? No sound of the fair. She got to her feet on a dusty white desert, a black sky overhead. She tried to speak, to yell, nothing. Her dollar had flown her to the moon.

There wasn't much to see besides dunes and craters. What was she supposed to do here? It was like the black and white pictures in the astronomy schoolbook, except for the tree.

It stood against all the shadows of outer space. Holding onto a bare branch was an old friend of hers. It was only a short walk away. She knew the second she played that guitar, everything would change.

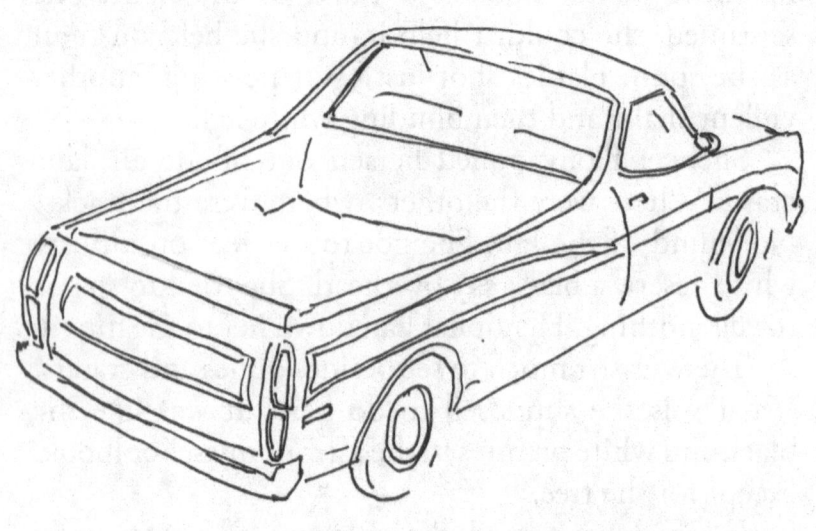

EL CAMINOS

Fatherly advice was the last thing Jay needed from him, but he knew it was coming and Jay wasn't surprised when it arrived. The old man didn't have much to give his son besides a lot of words. And like so much of those, this latest gift was just as absurd. Jay held in his hand the key to a rusted 1975 El Camino parked in the driveway.

"You'll see," his father told him and patted the orange hood, "In a few years the price for this will double!"

Jay was done with school now and he had his first place, a room above the garage of his landlady's house. His dad helped him make room for the car. Her cardboard boxes were labeled in stacks, a set of chairs, a sewing machine and more to discover.

Jay's father, who had an eye for such things, held up a coffeemaker and asked, "You think she wants this? What's she going to do with this old thing?"

"I don't know. She said to move all her stuff into the basement."

"I'm pretty sure she wouldn't miss it."

"Dad…"

"If it was something she wanted, she'd be using it. That's all I'm saying."

It took an hour and a half to get everything cleared out. Jay never did see that coffeemaker reappear and his father was in a hurry to get going once they were done. Jay wondered what he might find in his father's truck if he took a peek in the window. He didn't want to know. His arms were sore. Somehow he had ended up doing most of the moving.

And the car had a new home. "It's a classic!" his father told him, eyes shining in the dim garage. Now it was Jay's. The open bed of it held an inch of dark water. It smelled like a pond. Jay wondered if he would hear frogs when he got home later. His first night back from work and he would be sleeping over the Black Lagoon.

Jay rode his bike to the restaurant. He locked it to the tree by the kitchen door and went in for his shift. After five hours in the heat and steam, it was all he wanted to step into the dark outside and balance in the air and feel the cool rushing breeze like a bird let free from a cage. The backstreets were empty, the thin wheels hummed. In a couple minutes he was back in the driveway, stopped before the garage. What was he supposed to do with a car? His world was small enough his bicycle took him wherever he needed to go.

Opening the side door with a key, he pushed the bike into the peaty black of the garage and flicked the light switch to his left. 50 watts was enough to throw shadows, paint Vincent Price bruises of color and illuminate two El Caminos cramped together in the gloom.

"What?!"

He let his bike lean against the wall. The second car seemed to be a shade of blue or purple, it was hard to tell. It was in no better shape though; in fact it seemed to have been beaten around quite a bit more, an escapee from a junkyard chain-gang. A glinting crack thin as a switchblade wound slashed across the windshield. Jay sighed. He knew what happened, he knew who did this.

The rented room upstairs didn't have a phone. His landlady said he could borrow hers, but not at this hour, it was near eleven. The payphone outside the neighborhood market was his next stop. He dimmed the 50 watt moon and the El Camino graveyard returned to darkness.

Back in the night, Jay walked three blocks to Elizabeth Street. He took a swing at a sunflower. Its broad face was just the right height. It was so typical he would end up running down a mess like this. Gradual as a long distance moth, he arrived under the light on the corner.

The market was already closed. He dialed and waited, staring at the buzzing neon Rainier sign while the phone rang.

"What is it?" his dad answered.

"Did you bring me another car?"

"Yeahhh." A baseball game was on the radio in the background.

Jay tried to control his temper, "I don't want it! One car is already enough."

"No, no! You got to have two. You need one for parts."

"Parts?"

"Sure, that car's a classic but parts are hard to find. Now you don't have to worry. Hold on—"

Jay heard nothing but the loud baseball game. The surf sound of the crowd roared as the announcer set the scene. Would someone named Williams steal 2nd base?

"Dad, I can't stuff her garage with cars."

"Hold on—"

Williams got back just under the throw.

"I'll talk to you later, Dad." Jay replaced the receiver in its chipped plastic cradle. He didn't realize he would be returning to the phone booth in ten minutes. He didn't know there were three more El Caminos in the driveway, parked before the garage doors. They were worse than rabbits.

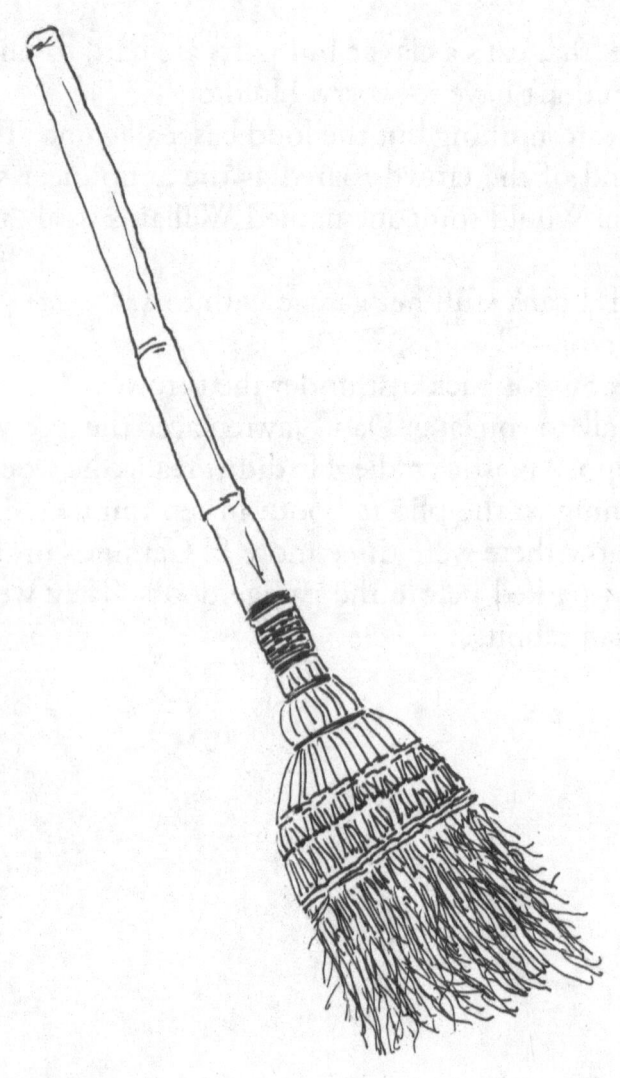

THE MEANEST PARENTS EVER

After shutting the door snugly on the attic, her father called through the ceiling to her, "Do you see any rats?"

"No!" she called back.

"Well keep looking!" was his muffled reply.

On her hands and knees, she crawled across the thick carpet of insulation. The weak flashlight made a Halloween scene. The roof, sloped just inches over her, held crypt bones of joists and beams and underneath her the snowy crunch.

Further underneath, in the living room below, her parents followed her progress with brooms, rapping the hard handled ends on the ceiling.

"See any rats yet?" her mother cried.

"No!" their daughter sounded from another realm.

She had reached the end and she stopped below the air vent set in the gable. She shined the light on its bent metal surface. The air around her now was flecked with choking insulation dust, forcing her to breathe into her crooked sleeve.

The brooms beat beneath her again and she answered, "No!" to them.

She thought about the vent, about prying it loose and trying to get through. If she could and if she could inch safely across those rain wet shingles to the bone white tree that leaned against the house, then she could get down and run.

The brooms cracked and this time she did see them. The rats were huddled in the corner in a shredded nest, eyes watching her the same way she watched the creatures who drove her up here. What was she supposed to do now that she found them? They were tucked in their bed, they were terrified. "It's alright," she whispered. "You're just babies, aren't you? I won't hurt you."

"We believe you."

That voice made her jump. She turned the pale glow and stopped her flashlight on a rat standing on its back legs watching her.

"We have no quarrel with you." Another rat stood behind the one who spoke. She guessed they were the babies' parents. They had that storybook look to them. Not like her parents though.

In the dim spotlight, she saw they had been working on something pinned to the cedar slats, a scrap of paper that had been drawn on. At first she thought it was one of her pictures, torn from a notebook. Did the rats have a museum up here devoted to her art?

"What is that?" she asked.

The rats looked at each and conferred too quiet for her to hear. Then the mother (she guessed that's who it was) took hold of the paper and passed it to her.

The poor girl couldn't believe her eyes. Written in big letters at the top was WANTED. Below that was a crudely drawn picture of her parents.

Another couple of thuds came from below and, "What's going on up there?"

"I'm still looking!" she shouted back at her parents. Then she asked the rats, "Is this them?"

The rat mother nodded. She brushed her eye, "We couldn't take it anymore."

"But what are you going to do?" whispered the girl.

"They're already being taken care of," said Mr. Rat. Yes, he was the father, she could tell by his vest and bowtie. He blinked in the dull light, "As we speak."

A crash downstairs, her parents yelled, and it sounded like a tornado for a moment. Then it was quiet.

"What happened?"

Mrs. Rat said, "That would be the bear."

"We called an exterminator," her dapper husband explained. "Oh," he said, as the girl began to turn, "I wouldn't go down there yet."

"No dear." Mrs. Rat placed her paw on the girl's hand, "Stay with us just a bit longer."

Mr. Rat agreed, "You don't want to interrupt a

bear when it's eating."

In the girl's imagination, that terrible vision was set like the stage of a play. It wasn't unusual for a girl her age to think thoughts like that about her mean parents, but having it actually happen made her shiver. Mercifully, there were no sounds of agony. The house below the attic was silent as the moon.

"That's it..." Mrs. Rat patted the girl's finger. The fine thread of her sweater brushed the girl's skin like a mosquito. "I think it's over now." Her husband nodded. He wore the tiniest pair of glasses.

The orphaned girl turned herself around with effort, bumping her head on the low ceiling.

Father Rat winced, "Careful sweetheart!"

"I'm okay," she told them. She crept back the way she had come, following the weakest flashlight beam. A candle would have been better; a match would have been an improvement. The rafters creaked as she made her way to the small door at the end of her journey. For a moment as she pressed on it she worried her father had latched it from the other side. That wouldn't surprise her. But it was only stuck. It burst open when she pushed both hands against it. Light splashed her and with it fresh air. She hung in the doorway catching her breath.

Going down the ladder, she looked over her shoulder, expecting to see a battlefield. It was nothing of the sort. The room was the same as she left it, only no mean parents in sight and a big bear sitting in her father's chair reading the *Herald*. It didn't notice her despite all the noise she must have made. Holding to the ladder she wondered if she should keep going down, but where else could she go? Not back to the attic. Anyway, he didn't look like a terribly ferocious bear. He wore a thick red plaid coat, the kind you would wear hunting in the woods. He turned the newspaper page and continued to read.

She got all the way to his side before he noticed her.

"Oh, hello," he greeted her, staring over the paper. "I'm Hank."

"I'm Ruth." She was covered in the pink down of insulation.

He lowered the paper and said, "What's that?" cupping his brown furry ear, "I'm a little deaf."

"My name is Ruth."

He nodded and apologized sincerely about her parents. "I was just doing my job, you know."

"What am I going to do without parents?"

"You don't have to worry about that, Ruth."

"I don't?"

"Look behind you," he pointed a claw.

She turned around. At the bottom of the ladder, the rat family had disembarked, father and mother holding suitcases, their children gathered next to them holding on shyly. Mrs. Rat clasped her hands as she looked the room over and happily exclaimed, "This is *so* much nicer than the attic!"

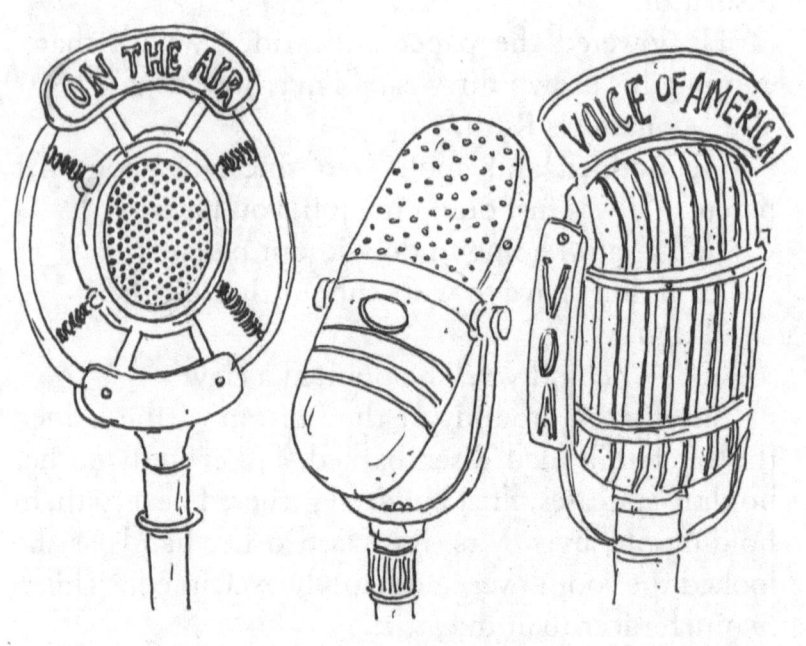

SILENT MOVIE STARS

I.
Cinderella

Lester Fremont was in trouble. For the first time, the movie-going audience heard his voice and it didn't go well. The boos and guffaws got louder each time he returned to the screen to speak. He sounded like a frog. But that was nothing compared to the reaction his costar Victoria Hasbitt received.

She was one of the luminous stars, like Louise Brooks and Lillian Gish.

But her voice was so uniquely pitched she came out of the speakers like a flock of geese. When she told the shoemaker, "I cannot tell a lie! If I do, I turn into a pumpkin!" the words brought tears of laughter to the El Rey Theatre in Albuquerque. "Even the children were laughing at me," she later sobbed to her maid.

After just ten minutes the director ordered the film be stopped. You couldn't even hear the piano in the orchestra pit. DeWitt Nimmley stomped out of the chaos with his crew at his heels. Lester was right behind him and heard him mutter, "Albuquerque..." in the foulest way.

It was common practice to show test reels at out of the way theaters. If the sneak peek was bad it was hoped the news would be contained in that town like a bug in a jar. Albuquerque was a big mad hornet.

Nimmley assured everyone this picture would be the Spectacle of 1928. How could it go wrong? A musical version of *Cinderella* starring Victoria Hasbitt and Lester Fremont was money in the bank. But ten minutes was enough; it was clear Nimmley's masterpiece was doomed. "We'll reshoot it!" he bellowed as he got in a taxi. Worse yet, a Hollywood reporter who happened to know about the preview had seen it all fall apart and the next day *Cinderella* was panned by *Variety*. In the space of a week, people were calling Victoria: "Has Been", "Has bitten off more than she can chew" and even more hurtful, "Victoria Halfwit." She threw herself into her penthouse apartment and locked the door.

Lester was sitting in a barber chair, his face covered in lather. As he read that scathing review he asked the barber to leave his face alone, he could use the disguise. Who would bother a guy walking around

Sunset Boulevard with a shaving cream beard? Even with that disguise though, a delivery girl arrived with a telegram for him. It was from Nimmley. He wanted everyone at the studio tomorrow. Lester wiped the lather from around his mouth and croaked, "Louie, you better give me that shave after all."

Lester had to think of something to survive tomorrow. "Mr. Fremont shall forthwith be christened Mr. Frogmont," *Variety* proclaimed. He needed a new voice.

At Louie's orders, he sat back in the chair and tried to calm down. He breathed the barber's menthol, he listened to the radio and the steady scrape of the razor. When he was done, Lester asked through the hot towel on his face, "Hey Louie, you still got that friend with the talking doll?"

"Fes? What about him?"

"I need to see him."

Louie removed the towel and asked, "What for?"

"A business opportunity," Lester grinned. "Yes sir," he tapped his forehead, "He's going to get me out of this jam."

Across the city, up ten floors from the street, Victoria Hasbitt demanded her telephone. She had a plan of her own. She would make *Variety* eat its words.

II.
Lester Fremont Hires a Ventriloquist

The Avalon Theatre didn't open til the afternoon, but Lester went into the alley and tried the backdoor. He was surprised it was unlocked. He poked his head into the cool hallway and said, "Hello? Anybody home?"

In a moment, a befuddled fellow in overalls appeared.

Lester snapped a quick salute. "Hi Pops. I'm looking for Fes. He around?"

"Dressing room." The old man didn't seem to mind if Lester was an assassin or not.

Down the hall, next to a broom closet was where Fes holed up. Lester found the ventriloquist with his feet up, reading a little trade magazine. His dummy Milo T. Smiley was tossed over a chair.

"Fes? I'm a friend of Louie the barber. He sent me here."

"That old bloodletter?" The voice seemed to come from the chair.

"Now, now, Milo," Fes said, "We both know Louie is the genuine article."

The voice replied, "Yeah, I read that article in the *Herald*—Brain Wanted!"

"Fes..." Lester interrupted; he wasn't prepared for a routine, "I'm sorry, but I'm in a bit of a bind. I really need your help." Seeing the blank look Fes gave him, he quickly added, "I'll pay."

The puppet cried, "Now you're speaking his language!"

"Please, Milo! Let the man speak."

Lester stared at the slumped dummy until he decided it was safe to talk. "I don't think we've met before. Like you, I make my living as an entertainer. I'm in the pictures, I'm an actor." For the next half hour in that little dressing room, they talked it over, they came to an agreement and Lester slipped his wallet from his coat. As he thumbed through the money, counting it out, Milo T. Smiley cackled from his chair and the doll's eyes rolled giddily in his wooden head.

III.
On the Set

The next morning the cast and crew of *Cinderella* gathered on the set of a fairy tale castle. Not far from the wishing well, DeWitt Nimmley stood on a stepladder holding a red megaphone. He told everyone he wouldn't let Albuquerque or *Variety* or the wags on the radio stop the production. He believed in it. He believed in them. It was a rousing speech, one he had practiced all night until it roared like "The Charge of the Light Brigade." One last thing before he climbed down, he asked the stars Victoria Hasbitt and Lester Fremont to meet him by the beanstalk.

Nimmley tucked the day's shooting schedule under his arm and crossed to the far side of the room where a fantastic beanstalk was tied to the ceiling in front of a backdrop of clouds with a spot where you could see the world far below. Tiny houses, a path and a stream. He tapped his foot and waited for them to arrive. The whole movie filled the studio. Across from him was the ocean liner deck where Cinderella sings. He scowled at the thought of Hasbitt tackling that song. Fremont was no better. When they sang it would be Albuquerque all over again. Unless something could be done…He watched Lester bustle past a hay cart. Victoria appeared around a giraffe. Nimmley locked eyes on one, then the other, back and forth like a swordfight, again and again as they approached.

"Mr. Nimmley, sir," Lester began.

The director cut him off as he launched into his tirade, "Listen you prima donnas! I will not let you ruin me or this picture! Either you change or I—" his speech was derailed. He noticed the two stars brought company. "What is this? Who do you have with you, your agents?"

The great Victoria Hasbitt presented the woman standing behind her. "This is Edna Bergling. At my own insistence, I sought her out. She is my voice coach."

Edna took a step closer and DeWitt got a look at what she held by her side. "You brought a dummy?"

"No, no," Edna tsked, "My little friend accompanies me everywhere. This is Peter Pinestreet."

"I'm not shaking that thing's hand!" Nimmley hollered. "Who do you have with you, Les? A juggler? Someone you met at a séance?"

Lester was still in shock…Victoria had stolen his act.

"I'm Fes," Lester's ventriloquist popped before the director with his hand outstretched. "A pleasure to meet you, Mr. Nimmley."

"You got one too?"

"Oh," said Fes, "You mean Milo? He tagged along, didn't want to miss seeing the studio."

"Where's the girls?" the puppet rolled its eyes.

"Now, now, Milo."

Lester cleared his throat. In an even lower octave, he continued, "Fes here is also my voice coach, more than that actually. See, what we propose—to save this picture, as you say—we have Fes here speak my lines while I mime them."

Victoria gasped. "That's exactly why I acquired Ms. Bergling's services!"

IV.
The Age of Sound

Cinderella resumed.

They were picking up at the shoemaker's where Victoria had to tell Lester she couldn't tell a lie. It would prove to be a very difficult shoot. The ventriloquists were carefully hidden behind the worktable as close as possible to the two stars when DeWitt yelled, "Action!"

The first lines went perfectly, "I cannot tell a lie! If I do, I turn into a pumpkin!" You couldn't tell it wasn't Victoria's supple voice. Edna Bergling gave her finest performance in a tone warm and yes, mellifluous as a purr.

All that needed to happen was for Lester to pass her the magic shoes he had made for her and recite his line. But as his mouth began to move, someone else spoke. A grating, chiding insult, "That figures! Last time I saw a face like yours it was carved on a jack o' lantern!"

"You monster!" Victoria screeched and slapped Lester. His shoemaker's cap went flying.

"It wasn't me!" he croaked.

Then Peter Pinestreet piped up, "It was that woodchip you hired!"

"Watch it!" Milo warned, "Don't get overheated, you might catch fire!"

DeWitt Nimmley was frozen in his director's chair as Peter Pinestreet grabbed a saw off the workbench and shrieked, "I'll cut you in half!"

Fes barely ducked the waving saw, muffling his doll's mouth and cradling Milo in his arms.

"Cut!" DeWitt could finally shout.

"I'm trying! I'm trying!" Peter Pinestreet squealed, wildly slashing the saw. It took two boom operators to control the unruly puppet, separate it from the saw while Edna Bergling struggled to contain the struggling cloth arms.

DeWitt fumed and kicked his chair and threw his megaphone at a hapless sawhorse. He needed the cameraman and a girl with a cup of coffee to make him see reason. All was not lost. *Cinderella* could begin again. A team of writers worked overnight. Puffing a cigar, circling the table like a toy train, DeWitt Nimmley stalked and barked until dawn when the story resurfaced, drastically revised and recast: this time with Lester as the Frog Prince and Victoria as the Fairy Godmother's cat. For its two stars, it was a demotion, but it was also the beginning of a new career, one in which they would become legendary character actors well into the age of sound.

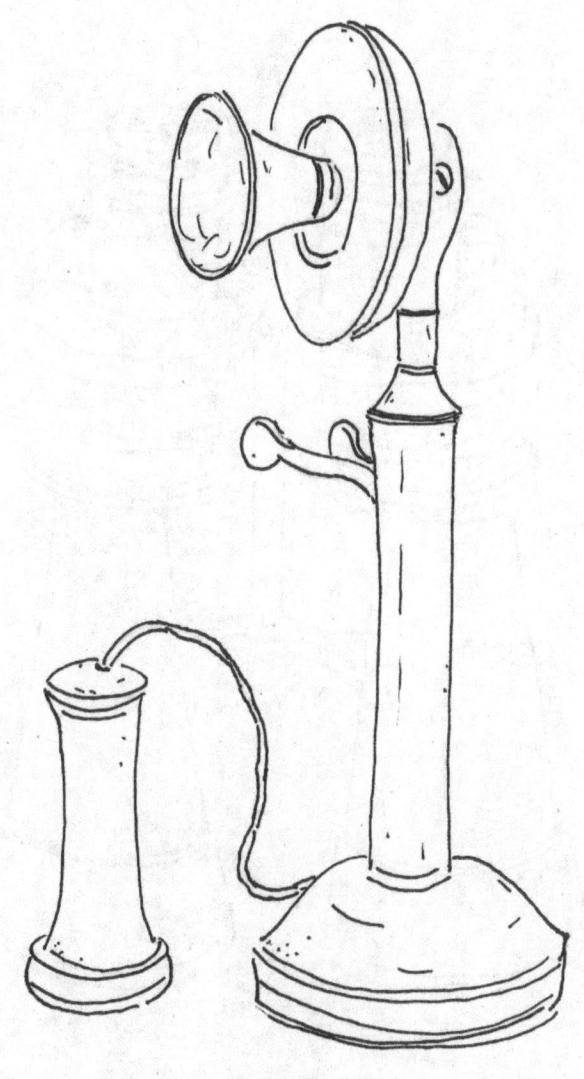

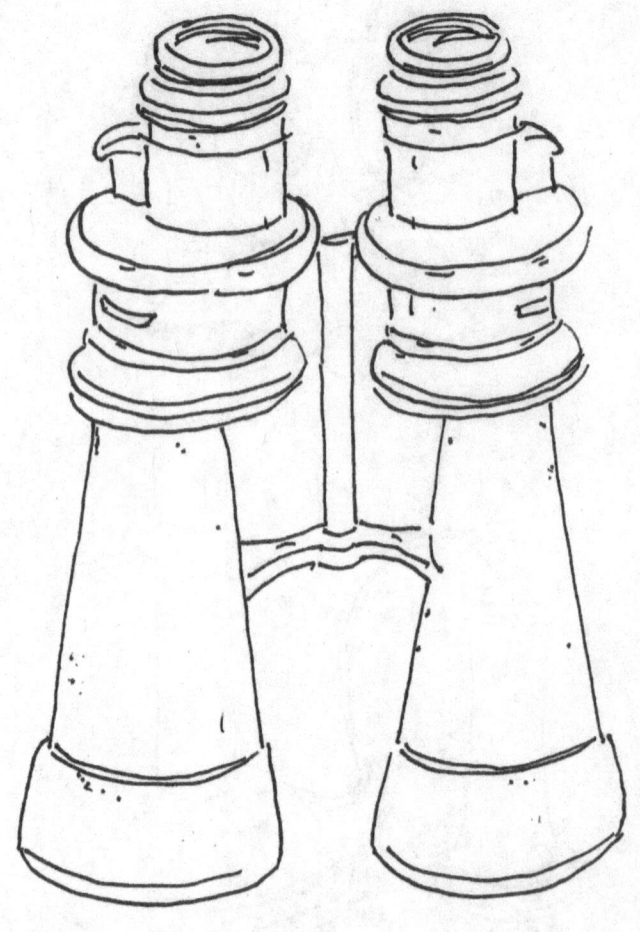

THE OLD SUBMARINE

My best friend in the 8th grade had a submarine. No, not really, but being with him it felt that way. We put to sea anytime we met. Once we came ashore in his backyard on a rainy day. It was windy too, leaves ran across the grass. He passed me a golf club and he took aim at the first hole, a plastic cola bottle cut in half. Up the side of a volcano, through a garden that had gone wild with weeds, doubling back to shoot through a bicycle wheel, a piece of gutter, a ramp made of brick, a toy car track, getting wet out there but we were used to the Seattle rain. That same yard was also the site of a secret rocket base. A catapult made from a strip of rubber attached to bungee cords staked to posts stuck in the ground. If anyone out there still bears the wounds of that day, I'm sorry. A Safeway bag full of oranges was our ammunition. First Emery demonstrated how each orange had to be softened by squishing it round and round, but careful not to split the skin. When it hit an unseen target far away it was sure to explode. One by one we sent every orange flying over the tall cedar fence. We could only imagine the carnage on the other side as we rained them down, splatting on driveways, car roofs, sidewalks and housetops.

Emery had a place on his floor for me anytime I wanted to sleep over. He had a poster in his room of Murphy's Law. It was probably meant for a saloon, a cartoon Irishman holding a big glass of beer, with a long list of deadpan hopeless humor scrawled beside him.

His younger brother's name was Cam. Cam would have fits and break things and had to be held down. Once he was done, only crying, Emery would let him go and Cam would run to his bedroom. I could hear him through the wall while we watched Steve Martin.

When their mother was home, she would hold Cam on her lap. She had a silk bathrobe that looked like a butterfly and she would laugh at our jokes. She liked to laugh. That was a family trait. When the Lake City Theatre had a Peter Sellers double-feature, she drove us there and bought popcorn too. It was fun to laugh with her. I don't know where the father was. I never asked. Everything was as it was.

They had to move around a lot. There were a couple years I didn't see him at all. Then, in high school he was back again. That old submarine took him to a new house. When I went there we would climb into the attic where he made a hideout. A light bulb on a string, silver cushions of insulation stapled to the slanted roof, sometimes we played Dungeons & Dragons, other times other games. I brought a box full of war, unfolding a map of Europe, with tiny airplanes. But my Luftwaffe was doomed, no matter how many Messerschmitts I put in the air, they were all shot down and my cities were bombed to dust. Cam distracted us, opening a door in the wall that held a cardboard box full of glossy magazines. A girl in a see-through raincoat, breathing became fluttery.

We had one class together senior year, but I barely saw Emery outside of that. Something was changing; he was submerged through mined harbors and scares I didn't know. You could hear the motor way back there pushing a propeller. Once he had a black eye and he wouldn't say how it happened. He was getting quiet these days, his smile was getting rare, old jokes were worn out. I noticed him with a girlfriend, between classes, talking in a serious way I never saw before. Someone told me she was pregnant. Another morning, just before class started, he showed up without a shirt. He sat next to me wearing his orange vest coat with his bare arms leaned on the desk. When he unzipped his coat, the realization was like a dreamer caught unaware. The teacher came over and said, "Maybe you'd like to go home, get dressed and come back." I went with him. We walked to his house and on the way back it started to rain. In a minute it soon became a monsoon. We were soaked when we arrived back at the school in time for the next class bell. Under the walkway, the girl I liked but never told laughed at me. I looked like I was washed off a deck.

    I saw Emery less and less. A strong current was at work pulling us apart, I was going one place and he was riding his bicycle further and further. He told me he was going to ride across America. When that became a story for the school paper, I was dazzled by the pretty reporter, made to make jokes about my old friend, telling her, "He'll never make it," meant as something funny, it was Murphy's Law, for these were the sunny last days of high school, everything was ending. Soon he would be pedaling up a mountain pass, descending the zigzag road into a thousand miles of summer ahead.

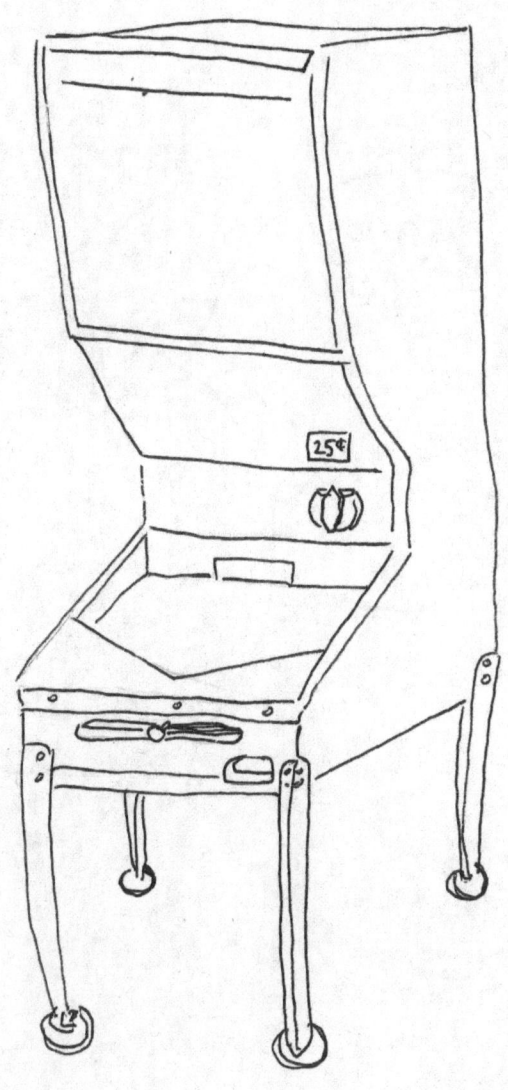

THE NEW APPLE TREE

It was election season and signs were on lawns, tacked to trees, taped to windows, bumper stickers. I joined the parade too, I couldn't help it. I was swept along by the electricity in the air. So I cut a piece of cardboard and painted it with Russian lettering that spelled FRIED POTATOES. I posted it on the sidewalk at the edge of our yard. I didn't expect anyone to know what it said, or what it stood for; it just seemed like the right thing to do. Wasn't I in for a surprise when twenty minutes later a car pulled up to the curb and parked. Two crusty looking men sat waiting on the front seat, smoking. The car looked as if it had been rolled up in someone's sleeve like a pack of cigarettes. I didn't know what to do. The engine coughed and smoke poured out like a cloud. They would glance at the sign and go on smoking. It was the same thing you see at Boomer's Drive-In, two guys in their car waiting for hamburgers. I really didn't know what to do, that crazy sign got me in trouble.

Now it's election time again, the same old scene, only I have become a little more restrained in my old age. I will vote of course but I don't really want to talk about it. I certainly won't be putting any more signs in the ground. That's what I thought, but as it turned out, I did.

I went to visit J. Genius who lives south of here. I took the highway to Exit 240 and got on Colony Road. When you leave the city, the trees turn into buffalo herds that reach far up into the hills. Houses are carved into them, mostly peaceful except for the appearance of a gigantic red white and blue billboard beside the road. It should have been a drive-in movie screen instead. I would have gladly parked in front of that to watch *King of the Zombies*.

This morning I read a poem about the way a wolf reacts to change. You move even an ashtray from its usual place and the wolf goes on the defensive. Something's wrong. I saw the same thing happen when I walked our dog. We have a shortcut we like, just past the elementary school. It cuts behind apartments between a rickety wooden fence and a corridor of blackberry vines. All of a sudden, Laika froze. Ahead of us, right in the middle of the path was something shocking. A cabbage! She stopped pulling the leash and froze. The fur on her shoulders bristled. The wolf in her was warning.

After a while, the road stops snaking and goes over a railroad track. A cow watched me. The asphalt ran out and the wheels rolled on dirt. I slowed way down as a dog trotted out to me. A woman who must have known I was due told me to follow the overgrown road going uphill. Road? It looked like it was knit from weeds and ferns. The car turned into a donkey and I rode it slowly upwards, making a tight turn.

Suddenly J. Genius filled the windshield waving a machete. He pointed me to a spot next to his pickup truck. I like getting out of the car onto earth not cement. You notice it right away. Also the view was out of this world. We were up high enough to see all of Samish Bay blue as the sky with the Anacortes refinery making clouds to the southwest. This is where he will be building his house.

He led me to the exact spot where a couple chairs

were set, around a card table beneath an old apple tree. This summer I've become a true fan of these wild apple trees and the crisp tart way they taste. They are relics of Rome, where farms used to be. Or maybe someone tossed a core up here long ago, or who knows maybe it was Johnny Appleseed passing by.

J. Genius told me about all the different animals living around here. I could see why they would all love it here. A breeze rushed up through all the tall weeds and leaves, sea warm and calm and somewhere out in the woods nearby was a mountain lion. A cedar chirped as it creaked. Some birds, small as Christmas lights, hopped from branch to branch. Talking, as it often does, led to concerns for the election. That conversation builds on its doom like the blueprint for a guillotine. It's a dark thing that needs to drop. While I ate one of the apples, he told me their new house will be built in this spot. He hated to say the tree will have to go. Its days in this spot are numbered. It hurts to have to know. There were more apples on the ground.

I tossed my core and made a wish. I had a vision of the future. The tree would die, the ground would be cleared and leveled, the cement foundation would be poured and the walls would go up. It would take a while for the seed growing underground. But next spring it will happen. While they're sleeping, the trunk will push the floorboards, fold them aside like origami, and by the time they wake up in the morning that apple tree will be stretching out its branches just like before.

OTHER FLAVORS

Thomas Felix tapes movies off TV and sells them. He got by. He lived in the student ghetto downhill from the university, off of 17th Ave under the edge of the garden in a basement room. It wasn't much: a twenty year old box-spring mattress, a coat hanger rod mounted by the window, a chair and his work table. The surface was piled like a city skyline with electronics, letters and paper towers, boxes full of videos. This was the headquarters of Thomas Film Classics Library.

At first, he taped the late-night movies and the ones shown in the afternoon after the news. People who had to be at work when *The Big Sleep* played would order their copy from him. Over the years he had a notebook full of customers. Every Sunday he checked the TV listings in the *Herald* and planned out the week. If he had a special order for *Flying Down to Rio* he would look for that. If *The Lost Continent* was on at 1 AM, he would catch it. He didn't just deliver a two hour recording though. The commercials for car lots and quack medicines were seamlessly edited out, his films looked as close as possible to the originals. All that was good training for his next step, a new direction. He wanted to put something else on tape. What if he redirected *Dark Victory*? What would happen if Bette Davis didn't die at the end? Couldn't he shuffle the pieces, make other things happen? Imagine *King Kong* with the ape getting free and paddling a freighter back to his island. Then he found a whole other channel, one from another planet actually.

By some stroke of luck, Thomas was the first person to tune into Martian television. He bought the weird looking contraption from a down-on-his-luck Martian who needed rocket fare to get back home. That was two years ago. Now Thomas made his living with the strange receiver. He was no longer interested in the cinema of this world. He got up at 8 and worked until 5, and each day was a marvelous discovery.

To be honest, Thomas didn't even know if he could describe these as movies. Nobody had seen anything like them before. They didn't seem to follow any story line, colors and sounds spun in seeming disarray, it was his job to reel them all together. And he loved it, he would get lost in it. As he worked, there was no recipe he followed, it was a feeling, he let himself go, opened up to some other guidance. Maybe it was hypnosis. Oftentimes he remembered those commercials for miracle medicine that used to clog the midnight movies he taped. If he was blind, he felt he could now see.

This was a good morning—he completed his 43rd tape. Because of the vast distance of outer space, he never knew when the next one would land. The inspiration kept him busy. They filled boxes and spilled across the desk. He tried all kinds of titles. It really didn't matter though, there was no way you could describe the movie. Currently he was using a combination of animals and colors. *Squirrel Gray* was printed on the top label, along with the recommendation: "These films may be best viewed on the small screen." In other words, he didn't expect to find them on the screen at the Avalon.

The telephone in the common room rang. He could hear it through his door. He could also hear Antoine making some loud meal, drop a spoon in a pan and stomp to the phone. "Hello?"

Thomas listened.

"Just a minute, I'll see if he's in." Footsteps to his door and a knock, "Phone call…"

"Okay," Thomas said. He left *Squirrel Gray* perched on a jar of instant coffee. The door opened into a kitchen, what his landlady also called the common room, maybe because it had a couch slumped against one wall. You were welcome to sit there and read the *Little Nickel* want ads someone left folded on the arm. "Thanks, Antoine." The phone was on the kitchen counter next to a can of chili and a bag of bread. He took the receiver and answered, "Thomas Film Classics."

Antoine stirred his chili and eavesdropped. None of the tenants knew exactly what Thomas was up to. It may have been something less than legal but whatever it was, it wasn't making Thomas rich; he was still renting a room in a basement. Antoine took the pan off the burner when it began to bubble.

"Yes," Thomas said, "I know where that is. I can be there in 20 minutes if that works?"

Antoine spooned his lunch noisily into a bowl. He glanced at Thomas hurrying from the counter. He didn't ask, he knew what Thomas would say—nothing—but one of these days Antoine expected to know what was going on. Some fine day in his mind there would be police and reporters and Antoine would be spotlighted for television and quoted on the front page of the *Herald*.

A couple waited for Thomas, sitting in a blue plastic booth at the International House of Pancakes on Brooklyn Avenue. Silent, still, watchful, wearing pressed and ironed suits, they resembled Sears manikins. They both had plates in front of them and cups of coffee but they only stared at the door. They had been waiting for two years.

When Thomas arrived, they both knew it was him. You couldn't watch Martian TV without it leaving its mark on you. Thomas stood by the podium scanning the room. He told the greeter that a woman and a man were going to meet him for lunch and she smiled, "They're already here, Mr. Felix. Follow me please."

She seated him at the booth and the couple waited until they were alone before they spoke.

"You are Thomas Felix?" the man asked.

Thomas said, "Yes, that's me."

The woman spoke next, "And you have in your possession a Martian television?"

Thomas held his breath. Suddenly he felt like bolting. Who were they? How did they know?

"Can I get you started with some coffee, sir?" A waitress stood beside Thomas. She slid a menu in front of him.

Across the table from Thomas, the man said, "Please bring him a coffee and whatever meal he would like."

"Our treat," the woman added.

"Oh, that's fine," the waitress nodded. As she left, Thomas had his last chance to escape, he almost did.

"You don't have anything to worry about," the man said.

"We are here to compliment you."

"It's an honor to meet you."

The way they timed their speech back and forth was almost mechanical.

Thomas stuck around, he didn't have the energy for a mad run through IHOP. Besides, the offer of a free meal was hard to resist. "What's going on?" he managed to ask.

The couple looked at each other briefly and the woman began, "We had to make sure it was you. We've seen the movies you made from our programming."

"We've been watching you," her companion continued, "All of Mars has been watching."

"Your movies are, to use an Earth phrase, 'the bees' knees' on our planet."

It dawned on Thomas. He was about to speak when the waitress arrived again with a copper pot of coffee and a cup. "Here you are, sir."

"Thanks," Thomas said. His hands went around the cup immediately.

"Have you decided what you'd like to order?"

"No," Thomas darted a look at the slick menu. "Not yet."

"I'll give you time," she smiled. "I'll be back."

Once she was gone, Thomas whispered, "You're Martians?"

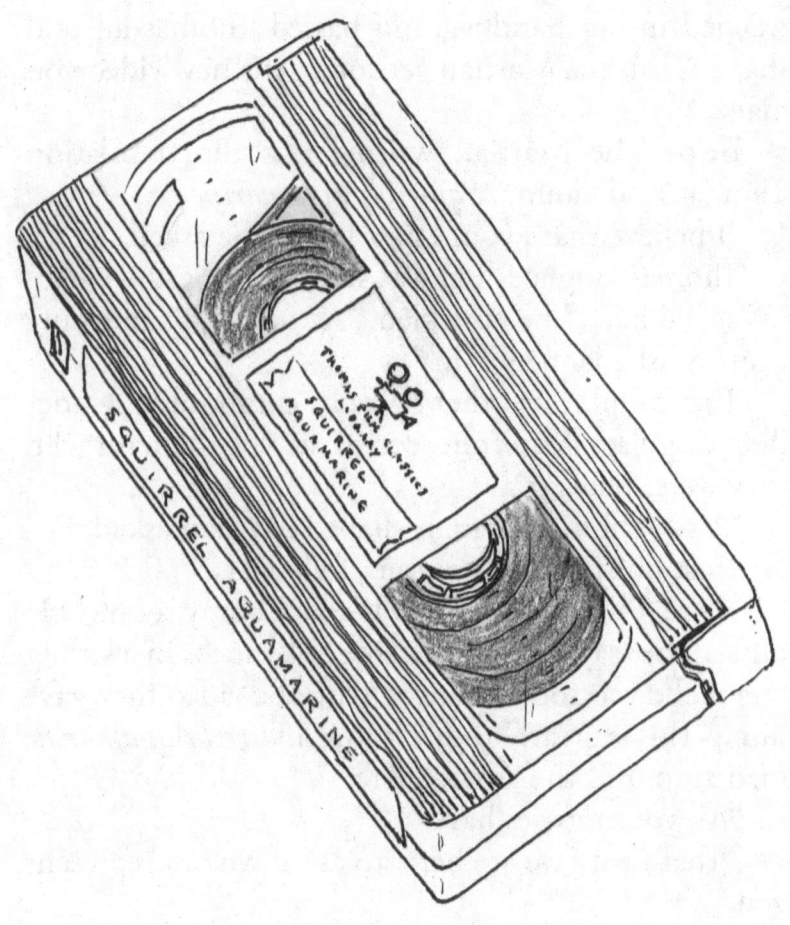

"Yes."

"We are."

"You may have this gift we brought." The woman reached in her handbag and passed Thomas an odd shape. "This is a Martian version of the new video you made."

Below the Martian writing was the translation Thomas read aloud, "*Squirrel Aquamarine.*"

"I believe that's your latest film?" she asked.

Thomas laughed. He was still admiring the video. "Well I'll be…" he chuckled. "Actually, this morning I just finished a new film."

The couple lost their plastic composure. Under their disguises, for a split second, he saw them for who they were. Flowers?

"A new film?" the man-shaped Martian asked.

"Just finished?" his partner followed.

"Sure. I'll get you a copy. It's back at my room." He missed the way they rustled like hollyhocks in a strong breeze, he was too entranced with the video they gave him. "This is great. I didn't know *Squirrel Aquamarine* made it out of the atmosphere."

"All your movies have."

"That's why we are here, to ask if we can represent you."

It was all happening like a dream; Thomas supposed he could fly if he tried. Of all things, he was thinking of Lana Turner at the counter of Woolworths in 1936 when a Hollywood agent discovered her. The waitress broke his trance.

"Have you decided yet?"

Thomas jumped. "No…I forgot to look." He picked up the menu and stared at the pictures, "I don't know…"

"That's alright. You can give me a signal when you're ready. Ma'am, sir? Are you not pleased with your meals?"

The two Martians had the same answer for her, "We prefer other flavors."

WILD BIRDS

"Come here," he said. "Let me show you something." Dilly took me past the front steps towards the open garage. I was expecting another one of his stories: thieves have taken bicycles out of there before and what about the time someone broke the chain on his freezer and stole a whole flat of blueberries. On it goes. If that garage could only talk, what a despairing tale it would tell. He grabbed the shoebox on top of the piano and lifted the cardboard lid. I don't know what I was expecting, but the sight of the dead blue jay was startling. Birds are supposed to be in the sky.

"My neighbor shot it," he said, "right out of the pear tree, right over there."

I've been noticing those blue jays this week, they've been active, picking up green acorns, soaring across the road, topping the oak tree and calling from the telephone wires, squawking, sounding like they might be part of some electricity output with the blue gas flame that rises on their head. Of course they are loud birds, alarm clocks that are just out of reach. Anyone who pays attention to birds knows what they are like but why would someone shoot one?

Dilly already called the police and told them what happened, how it could have been him, how he was standing by the tree when it happened. These days the police are under stress too. The police seem less likely to venture. After he lost his temper with the officer, Dilly was transferred. He gave the phone to his wife and Luanne was switched to Fish and Wildlife Services. They told her yes, it's illegal to kill any wild birds. The only ones the law doesn't apply to are sparrows, starlings and pigeons. They said they would send someone to the scene of the crime. That was hours ago.

We are all under stress. These are the times we live in.

. Walking over here, my mind was somewhere else, all this is happening while we are selling our 1978 car. This week, Dilly has been a help getting it started again. Opening the hood, using an eyedropper of gasoline, he filled what turned out to be the bulb for the window washer fluid. It wasn't the fuel pump, but maybe it irritated the car enough because yesterday we got it going. This morning the car was dead again, the last gasp of 1978.

Compared to all that car stress, a bird of distraction was welcome.

I carried his battery charger and as we crossed the street another neighbor called out to us. Bess waved from the top of the driveway. One of Dilly's amazing traits, besides being a professed backyard mechanic, was the unhurried way he would cross a street. In his mind, this is still the rural road of 1961. Occasional Ford Falcons and pickups ferry between the truck farms that sprout along 32nd. He wears jeans and a white t-shirt, he works at Joe's Garden and spends his paycheck on Royal Crown colas pulled from the icebox at the market.

Bess asks if we'd like some cucumbers. Of course, I can't pass that up, fresh from a roped off section of her yard. She gives me three and the green little horns rough my arms. We admire her garden, protected from the deer, and for a minute or so we talk about that. Every year the hydrangea has to be cut back. She needs a hand stepping free from the pile of cut limbs. While she holds Dilly's sleeve, he talks about the hibiscus seeds he brought back from Iowa that he planted this summer. He can give her some. Their chatter reminds me of the two birdwatchers I met in the woods. I was walking the dog and this couple was on the edge of the path holding binoculars. I asked them about something troubling me, "Lately I haven't heard the birds waking me up at 4 AM. Is that natural? Are they okay?" "Yes," the woman assured me, that was their season, they have moved on. Just like the Byrds' song, "Turn, Turn, Turn," I'll have to wait for next year to hear their morning radio.

Then Dilly tells Bess his blue jay story and the tragedy is traveling now like a runner of wisteria.

"There's a pair that I see every day." She points a saw at the songbird feeder filled with seed and peanut shells for the jays.

Dilly said, "Well, now there's one less to feed." He tried to laugh but it isn't a pleasant thought.

Who would shoot a blue jay? It had to be a kid, right? I remember when I got a BB gun and I went hunting with a friend. It only lasted a minute. A camellia full of flowers and sparrows. Each one we shot, another would hop next to it to check on it and soon the air was a shriek and there were a lot on the ground. That's when I stopped shooting birds. It was too much like murder.

The sky is a room that has one less bird. You can't go to the department store and buy another blue jay off the rack to put back on the branch it fell off.

Once a bird is gone it's gone.

The charger didn't work on the battery. Dilly and Luanne came back at dusk and we tied a mountaineering line to the bumper and pulled the car down 32nd until the engine jumped into gear. That seemed to suit it fine. I drove to the station on the corner and filled the gas tank. What more could a car want?

The next morning the car started and I backed it out onto the street in front of our house. Behind me I could see the orange road signs. The loss of our country life is happening, there are bulldozers clawing up the north end of 32nd and more construction on the other end too. Huge gray trailer trucks roar back and forth. We're squeezed in the middle, the last of a legacy of farm houses, poplars and apple trees, old wooden fences staked in this soil rich valley. I don't understand. Do they want to fill in the whole street with a corridor of those cardboard towers? Who are all these people they're calling in like swallows to fill their hives?

I came back out at 9:45 and started it again. I have to admit I'll miss the feel behind the wheel, but it's going to a better place, new owners are looking forward to it. They arrived in 15 minutes to take it away. We signed the title paper, put in more coolant and oil for its maiden voyage and then of course it wouldn't start. If it was an animal you'd swear it didn't want to leave. Its wheels were planted, the engine would only growl. Jonas spent 5 hours working on his new used car. I got out of his way and let him work. He knew what he was doing, he knew there was something simple he was overlooking. I watched from our window. Halfway to him I could see a snail. It stood out like a bolt. The snail has been on the fencepost all morning long, unmoving, waiting, thinking or sleeping or waiting to think about sleeping.

Jonas was right, it was simple. He found a burnt fuse. Once he replaced that, his car was ready and he started it up and drove it away into the 21st Century. We put feelings into things like cars, I don't know why, that shouldn't be. They have wheels, that's all, and this one was meant to leave. I should be thinking there goes one less worried dream.

I walked up the driveway and sat by the window inside the house.

Cars go past on the street. There's no sign of the sky. Because of the forest fires the air has become a smoggy gray fog. It's thick enough to turn the sun into a dull penny above the pear tree. Think of the water in a murky pool where an orange carp hangs just below the surface.

A blue jay left the oak tree. It had to fight to keep itself airborne, dip and flap and dip again above the leaf covered lawns.

After a while, I decided I would go across the street to Dilly's house.

I looked both ways. I guess I'm not as trusting as Dilly. To my left, the orange ROAD CLOSED AHEAD signs, to my right a long dusty shot at the end of 32nd. These days there's less traffic: one good thing about all the construction, people are taking other routes. The other morning I saw a snail taking its time crossing the road.

I coughed. We have to wear masks to breathe the air.

I glanced in the garage where he dares the modern world to remember the golden rule and followed the concrete path. As I knocked on the door, Otis barked, shadows moved behind the screen then Dilly appeared and told me, "I buried the blue jay." There would be no Perry Mason inquest, no evidence presented before the court of a murdered innocent bird, wings folded like a dead Prussian soldier. Luanne showed behind him as I gave him a hug.

Thank you for all your help, I told them, we couldn't have done it without you. We have to stick together, with all these things happening we need each other. These are still the old days when people help each other out. Luanne says obviously, "That's what neighbors are supposed to be!" I hope that part of us continues, that whatever silver robot future awaits us, people will still be like that. Come on everyone, it's not that hard to figure out!

I checked up and down 32nd and I crossed when it was safe. On the other side, I looked back. Next door to Dilly and Luanne's, I saw their neighbor's house. That was where it started. A gunshot. Three people in blue uniforms were on the roof. Weightless as astronauts they hopped along the slant and then one of them, apart from the rest, stopped on the sunlight and let out a scream.

MARVELOUS MARVIN'S UNREAL ESTATE

I'm the Marvelous Marvin you've heard about. The one on the TV commercials talking a mile a minute like someone selling used cars. Only I'm not peddling Buicks and Fords, I'm selling your very own slice of Himalayan peak, or a hammock on a tropical beach, or a cave full of diamonds under a pavement lot. I sell unreal estate.

Well, I did. I made a good living that way. At least I had everything I thought I could ever want.

But I stopped. I have every intention of becoming a different person. I'm done with the office, the hours and paychecks, the fast paced rat race and especially I'm done with all that talking.

Now I've taken a vow of silence.

This will come as welcome news to those who are tired of my voice, sick of me interrupting their late night monster movies and detective shows. For this I apologize. I'll be quiet now.

You won't see Marvelous Marvin on TV anymore but I'm still on the air.

I live in a seventy foot tall dandelion. A spiral staircase runs up the stem to the yellow petal house at the top. As you would imagine, it gives me quite a view of the neighborhood. Any taller and I would see all the world. Don't suppose it's my intention to sit on a throne, king of the town, I just needed to get up and away from the ground. Here I feel like I'm a low floating cloud, alone with my thoughts.

I didn't know if I was done with wonders, but after I turned my room into a dandelion I had a new vision for the world around me. I got tired of watching the trucks going back and forth delivering bulldozers and cranes and building concrete blocks on my street. I decided it was time for unreal estate to return. Not like before. Marvelous Marvin's Unreal Estate has gone underground. Nobody knows that down by the water I transformed the apartments into a row of 19th century Amsterdam. The street is cobbled, a lamplighter shows up at dusk every night.

That was only the beginning. Some things are small as a 1910 wheat penny dropped on the sidewalk. My latest creation is a forest in the parking lot of Food Giant. I might have gone too far though. Food Giant is complaining on the news—shoppers lost the cars they parked there. A family trying to get to their station wagon was chased by wolves. They barely escaped back to the pavement. Old growth cedars blocked the lot. Ravens circle and call above.

The *Herald* tried to blame me but I'm not the only one with this ability. If Food Giant is unhappy with my forest they can get Cord Pepham to do what he does. He wrecks unreality. I don't want to put down his work, but if they commission Cord Pepham to replace that forest they'll end up with a murky pond for a parking lot. It takes a lot of effort for unreal estate. Not everyone can do it.

I get excited when I find someone else in my line of work. Something nice happened last week when I was out walking. My journey took me by an audience of Frankenstein heads in a yard. No, it's not my doing, it was not my tribute to Boris Karloff. It surely wasn't Cord either—he couldn't conjure anything so outrageously original. Sorry, Cord. They looked like monstrous green flowers planted along the sidewalk, thirty of them at least. Their eyes watched me approach. I was impressed. This may be the work of an amateur unreal estate agent, but there was no denying the genius of their little patch of ground. What joy to come across this place in front of this ordinary house along a stretch of road where nothing else tried to break the monotony of conformity. While I admired them a girl came outside and spoke with me. She recognized me from TV. I carry a handful of cards for moments like this. I showed her the one that explained that I don't talk anymore. Then I got a pencil and wrote a new message on the back, one that said how much I liked what she was doing. She gave me faith in the ones coming after me.

Anyone can do things to change reality. It just takes a little effort and creativity and daring. Look around, you'll see others like us. You should be able to sense it like finding music on the radio dial. We live in an unreal reality.

A perfect example is Charlie Chaplin. That's what I call him. From up here everyone looks like they're in a silent movie. The first time I saw him, he was bumbling up 32nd Street, stopping wherever flowers grew along the sidewalk. He picked from the cracked cement and overgrown lawns, never from gardens. I liked that idea of finding flowers. He was serious as a florist looking for the right one in the weeds. Then out of his coat pocket came a string tied to scissors and he would snip and add to the growing bouquet. A tangle of stems and yellow leaves, pale white petals and dandelions, it looked more like something you would offer to a goat than to someone you were courting.

I watched him turn down Maple Street and I got my binoculars so I could keep watching. He really had that Charlie Chaplin walk, brisk, feet almost paddling. He stopped at a door. All he needed was a cane to knock with. There was no answer though. He looked through the keyhole; he put an ear to the door. Finally he left the flowers. I had to wait a couple days before I saw him again. You could tell something happened. He carried an apple. It was cupped, almost hidden in his hands. At that same house, he stopped again but nobody was answering. You could tell what he was feeling. He left the apple on the windowsill. It looked like a cemetery prop. He could leave all the flowers and apples in the world, they weren't working prayers. I remember what it's like: love and heartache and poverty. I wanted to tell him, "You don't know how funny you are. Remember the way you pick flowers and run from bees." I didn't want him to suffer or see him sad; he moved down the alley like a raindrop. Then he turned a corner and disappeared from my binoculars.

    I've been looking for him since then. No sign. I was watching a movie I shouldn't interfere with. I had to let this play out like *City Lights*. Even with the powers of unreal estate there was nothing I could do to make his dream come true. Sure, I could create other worlds, but not with her. It's hard to see when things are over. He was made for other things happening far away. He needed a flying machine or a steamship or a Greyhound bus to take him there. At least I could do that for him. He would find a ticket in his coat pocket. It wasn't exactly my usual magic but it would work. One morning he would pack up his things in a paper grocery bag, walk to the station downtown and leave for a new world. From there he was on his own. That was the ending I put on it. He would be alright. Picture the petals closing around my house, folding for the night.

"How could you write that abominable book?"

"Oh darling, it was a hobby, an urge, like collecting butterflies."

—*Footsteps in the Dark*

AFTERWORD

This was the summer of the pandemic, forest fires, violence and cruelty, the empire's groaning collapse—since the pyramids and the Roman days we've been watching the signs, well aware of the way things fall apart—still the Marvel putters on. I caught these stories in the air and put them in this book the way you would capture lightning bugs in a jar:

The Puttering Marvel takes place in my grandparents' house in Maine. I spent a lot of time in their kitchen listening to stories, the big white oil stove, talking at the table, a cigarette smoking in the brass ashtray, the window with its view of the birds at the feeder. I loved the workshop and I loved to follow the mussel shells to the shore. The stove illustration is actually from a Seattle apartment where I lived for a while when I was a dishwasher, back when America was first bombing Iraq.

One late afternoon in August we gathered some friends around in the yard. Everyone wore a mask. I learned about the kushtaka and *The Broken Record* began to play.

I used to listen to a lot of 1950s music. You could still hear them on the radio and I had a lot of favorite songs. Those people who remember Buddy *Holly* were always waiting for him.

J. Genius told me his father advised him to invest in *El Caminos*. It didn't happen exactly like the story I wrote. The car in question was actually a Ranchero and he never got one.

I don't know how many accused parents have been awarded this title, probably a lot. No doubt about it, *The Meanest Parents Ever* is a tribute to Roald Dahl. We have had quite a bit of adventure over the years with rodents in our house and barn. I suppose this is also a tribute to them. Thanks for all the sleepless nights.

Back on a sunny day in early spring, I met Aaron for cat coffee and I told him about my idea for this story. *Silent Movie Stars* had to stew for a while, like the cat in the coffee urn before I got to it.

The Old Submarine is true to real as I can be. High school is a strange zoo. I don't know what happens to old friends, they stay floating in a bubble if you never see them again.

I knew *The New Apple Tree* was going to be a story. J. Genius is good at inspiring me, making sure of that. [See *Imaginary Someone* (2020) for more.] I drove there feeling it was going to happen, watching out the car window taking notes.

In my novel *Old Salt*, there's a chapter about Seattle's Brooklyn Avenue. *Other Flavors* picks up where the IHOP used to be. It was a great place to go after seeing a double feature at The Neptune Theatre, just around the corner. You got a copper urn of coffee that could last for hours. This is a story that ended up not the way I thought it would. The original notes I wrote for this story are another reality:

Magic Lantern Production House is a Martian Syndicate. They trick him into meeting at International House of Pancakes. He realizes they are gangsters working for Martians. Don't expect heroics. He was just trying to get by. Looks up at night sky, Mars a drop of rust sending out signals

Fortunately for Thomas Felix the story took a different turn.

Selling our old Volvo caused a stir in the neighborhood. *Wild Birds* is a sort of field recording. The car had been sitting in our driveway for a year and then suddenly it was time for it to take flight. Doing something you don't want to do that needs to be done anyway. 32nd Street is in a valley that used to be truck farms and our neighbor across the street remembers those days.

I thought *Marvelous Marvin's Unreal Estate* was going to be a novel, but it chose to be this instead. Stories know what they're doing, like poems they know what shape to take and when to stop.

THE PUTTERING MARVEL
Written by Allen Frost
Summer 2020

Illustration from *Home Recordings* (2009)

Books by Good Deed Rain

Saint Lemonade, Allen Frost, 2014. Two novels illustrated by the author in the manner of the old Big Little Books.

Playground, Allen Frost, 2014. Poems collected from seven years of chapbooks.

Roosevelt, Allen Frost, 2015. A Pacific Northwest novel set in July, 1942, when a boy and a girl search for a missing elephant. Illustrated throughout by Fred Sodt.

5 Novels, Allen Frost, 2015. Novels written over five years, featuring circus giants, clockwork animals, detectives and time travelers.

The Sylvan Moore Show, Allen Frost, 2015. A short story omnibus of 193 stories written over 30 years.

Town in a Cloud, Allen Frost, 2015. A three part book of poetry, written during the Bellingham rainy seasons of fall, winter, and spring.

A Flutter of Birds Passing Through Heaven: A Tribute to Robert Sund, 2016. Edited by Allen Frost and Paul Piper. The story of a legendary Ish River poet & artist.

At the Edge of America, Allen Frost, 2016. Two novels in one book blend time travel in a mythical poetic America.

Lake Erie Submarine, Allen Frost, 2016. A two week vacation in Ohio inspired these poems, illustrated by the author.

and Light, Paul Piper, 2016. Poetry written over three years. Illustrated with watercolors by Penny Piper.

The Book of Ticks, Allen Frost, 2017. A giant collection of 8 mysterious adventures featuring Phil Ticks. Illustrated throughout by Aaron Gunderson.

I Can Only Imagine, Allen Frost, 2017. Five adventures of love and heartbreak dreamed in an imaginary world. Cover & color illustrations by Annabelle Barrett.

The Orphanage of Abandoned Teenagers, Allen Frost, 2017. A fictional guide for teens and their parents. Illustrated by the author.

In the Valley of Mystic Light: An Oral History of the Skagit Valley Arts Scene, 2017. A comprehensive illustrated tribute. Edited by Claire Swedberg & Rita Hupy.

Different Planet, Allen Frost, 2017. Four science fiction adventures: reincarnation, robots, talking animals, outer space and clones. Cover & illustrations by Laura Vasyutynska.

Go with the Flow: A Tribute to Clyde Sanborn, 2018. Edited by Allen Frost. The life and art of a timeless river poet. In beautiful living color!

Homeless Sutra, Allen Frost, 2018. Four stories: Sylvan Moore, a flying monk, a water salesman, and a guardian rabbit.

The Lake Walker, Allen Frost 2018. A little novel set in black and white like one of those old European movies about death and life.

A Hundred Dreams Ago, Allen Frost, 2018. A winter book of poetry and prose. Illustrated by Aaron Gunderson.

Almost Animals, Allen Frost, 2018. A collection of linked stories, thinking about what makes us animals.

The Robotic Age, Allen Frost, 2018. A vaudeville magician and his faithful robot track down ghosts. Illustrated throughout by Aaron Gunderson.

Kennedy, Allen Frost, 2018. This sequel to *Roosevelt* is a coming-of-age fable set during two weeks in 1962 in a mythical Kennedyland. Illustrated throughout by Fred Sodt.

Fable, Allen Frost, 2018. There's something going on in this country and I can best relate it in fable: the parable of the rabbits, a bedtime story, and the diary of our trip to Ohio.

Elbows & Knees: Essays & Plays, Allen Frost, 2018. A thrilling collection of writing about some of my favorite subjects, from B-movies to Brautigan.

The Last Paper Stars, Allen Frost 2019. A trip back in time to the 20 year old mind of Frankenstein, and two other worlds of the future.

Walt Amherst is Awake, Allen Frost, 2019. The dreamlife of an office worker. Illustrated throughout by Aaron Gunderson.

When You Smile You Let in Light, Allen Frost, 2019. An atomic love story written by a 23 year old.

Pinocchio in America, Allen Frost, 2019. After 82 years buried underground, Pinocchio returns to life behind a car repair shop in America.

Taking Her Sides on Immortality, Robert Huff, 2019. The long awaited poetry collection from a local, nationally renowned master of words.

Florida, Allen Frost, 2019. Three days in Florida turned into a book of sunshine inspired stories.

Blue Anthem Wailing, Allen Frost, 2019. My first novel written in college is an apocalyptic, Old Testament race through American shadows while Amelia Earhart flies overhead.

The Welfare Office, Allen Frost, 2019. The animals go in and out of the office, leaving these stories as footprints.

Island Air, Allen Frost, 2019. A detective novel featuring haiku, a lost library book and streetsongs.

Imaginary Someone, Allen Frost, 2020. A fictional memoir featuring 45 years of inspirations and obstacles in the life of a writer.

Violet of the Silent Movies, Allen Frost, 2020. A collection of starry-eyed short story poems, illustrated by the author.

The Tin Can Telephone, Allen Frost, 2020. A childhood memory novel set in 1975 Seattle, illustrated by author like a coloring book.

Heaven Crayon, Allen Frost, 2020. How the author's first book *Ohio Trio* would look if printed as a Big Little Book. Illustrated by the author.

Old Salt, Allen Frost, 2020. Authors of a fake novel get chased by tigers. Illustrations by the author.

A Field of Cabbages, Allen Frost, 2020. The sequel to The Robotic Age finds our heroes in a race against time to save Sunny Jim's ghost. Illustrated by Aaron Gunderson.

River Road, Allen Frost, 2020. A paperboy delivers the news to a ghost town. Illustrated by the author.

The Puttering Marvel, Allen Frost, 2021. Eleven short stories with illustrations by the author.

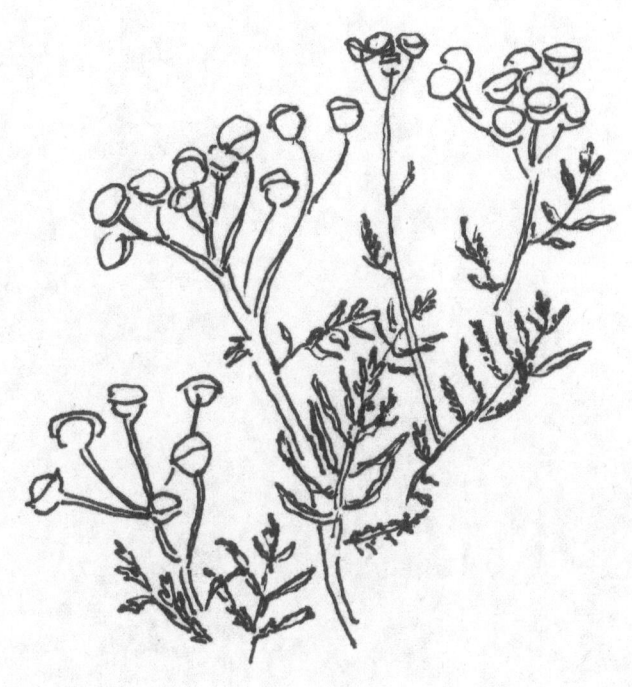

www.ingramcontent.com/pod-product-compliance
Lightning Source LLC
LaVergne TN
LVHW031540060526
838200LV00056B/4592